IN A WORLD

FAR, FAR AWAY

stories and observations from the students of 826CHI

In A World Far, Far Away
© by 826CHI

This book is a work of fiction. Names, characters, places, and incidents are either products of the authors' imaginations or are used fictitiously. Any resemblance to actual events or locales or persons, living or dead, is entirely coincidental. Or an instance of synchronicity, if you're looking for it.

Cover & interior illustrations: Grace Molteni
Book design: Waringa Hunja

Director of Programs: Maria Villarreal
Publications Coordinator: Waringa Hunja

Proceeds from your purchase of this publication support 826CHI, a non-profit creative writing, tutoring, and publishing center. www.826chi.org

The views expressed in this book are those of the authors and the authors' imaginations.

First Edition 826CHI 2018
Printed in the United States by McNaughton & Gunn

TABLE OF CONTENTS

FOREWORD

by After School Tutoring and Writing student ambassadors: Brandon A., Alondra M., Abigail M., Adolfo T., and Vanessa T.

We're so excited you picked up our book! In it, you'll find a collection of new stories that took a lot of imagination and creativity. Every story was a little bit difficult to write and some of us are a little nervous to share them with you but we also know that writing takes practice and we hope you'll have a great time reading!

We don't know if you've been published before, but it's a pretty big deal for us. We're scared and embarrassed because what if people don't like our stories or laugh at them? But we're also so grateful for the opportunity to be published authors and we're happy because our work usually gets graded and then goes in the trash or recycling but now we can keep our hard work forever in this book.

If you're inspired by our stories and you want to try writing, we'd like to give you some advice: Try writing about something that happened to you, even if you think it might be boring, because you can change the end and make it your own. Write about what you want, not for a school assignment. You're going to have to write and be creative in the future so you should learn now. Sometimes it won't be very fun, but you'll feel proud when you finish a story.

We'd love for you to read this book somewhere warm and comfortable, maybe in bed before you fall asleep so you can dream about the worlds we created. Feel free to skip around and read it in any order, but we recommend reading one or two stories a day so you can savor the book.

When you're done, we would really like it if you sent a letter to 826CHI (1276 N. Milwaukee Ave, Chicago) or tag us on social media (@826CHI on Twitter/Instagram) and describe your favorite part of the book! In the meantime, buy yourself a donut and happy reading.

THE VETERINARIAN PRINCESS

BY STEPHANIE M., GRADE 7

Once upon a time, there lived a princess named Karen. The kingdom was beautiful. It was full of magical creatures, but mostly unicorns. Her parents always wanted things just right. One day, they both went to find Karen. When they found her, they asked, "Karen, do you want to be the next queen?"

She said, "No, I want to be a veterinarian." They got so mad at her. They grabbed her by the hair and pulled her to the throne room and told her, "You will be the next queen whether you like it or not." A few weeks later, she started Royal and Veterinarian school.

Five years later, she was done with school. When they went to find Karen, they asked her again, "Do you want to be the next queen?" She said "NO, I do not. You can't make me. I want to be a veterinarian."

Karen and her parents had a huge argument. The king said, "Fine, if you want to be a veterinarian, leave the kingdom and never come back."

"Fine," she said. She packed up all her belongings and stole some money for a house and food. She finally found a home and she decorated it. Once it was finished, she was hungry so she went to the market.

On her way to the market, she saw a poster saying "Help Wanted". It was at an animal hospital. She went in and talked to the boss and she got the job.

A few weeks later, the king and queen were going to the market and saw a picture of their daughter on an Employee of the Month poster. They saw her coming out of the store and she finally saw her parents. Karen said, "Mom… Dad."

"Karen!" said the king and queen. "We are sorry. We were so greedy. Could you ever forgive us?"

Karen said, "Of course I will!" The three went to the market and lived happily ever after.

The End

A NORMAL DAY
BY ALDO A., GRADE 5

Professor Apple was doing an experiment in his big lab, but he needed a potato to finish his experiment to save humanity. While the big potato, PFC, was inside his own lab, he was planning an evil scheme to turn everyone into potatoes. However, all he needed was a potato. So they both went to the grocery store to get one, but there was only one more. They both put their hand on the potato. They got mad at each other and that is how it all started.

Professor Apple took PFC's potato, but PFC took Professor Apple's potato. So Professor Apple took it back.

Out of nowhere, PFC took it back so Professor Apple dug a tunnel to PFC's lair, but PFC trapped him! Professor Apple, however, was able to escape with the potato.

Eventually, after a long, long time, the potato melted so they both went to the grocery store to get another one. They both got a potato and created peace. After they got out of the store, they ran into Jake who is the protagonist. Jake had two lightsabers, three bombs, and orange hair. Jake thought Professor Apple and PFC teamed up, so he threw an exploding kitten and the potatoes turned into potato chips.

Professor Apple and PFC tried to catch as many potato chips as possible, but Professor Apple took all the potato chips and gave them to the bank. The bank accidentally ate them all so Professor Apple got so mad that he threw an exploding kitten and exploded the world.

THE FUNNY STORY OF BELL AND THE YELLOW BABY CHICKEN

BY ALONDRA A., GRADE 3

Once upon a time, there was a girl named Bell. Her father was an artist. But Bell had an admirer. His name was Gaston. He was mean to Bell's father, and he wanted to marry Bell. Gaston did not want anything more than to marry her.

Bell lived in a little house that was full of paintings. She had chickens. Every morning, she went to get the eggs to make breakfast. But then, one day, when she opened an egg, she screeched and ran to the living room and said, "Why is there a yellow baby chicken in the cold egg?" But the chicken was on the pan and the pan was on!

PENCILVANIA

BY ALESSANDRA T., GRADE 7

In a world far away (just kidding, it's two hours away, you can take a plane!), there was a place that will knock the lead out of your pencils.

It was called Pencilvania.

It was just a random day on Lead Street in the life of a girl named Angela. She had a twin sister named Angeline. There was a dog named Sparley who also lived on Lead Street--many said he was cute. Angela was the neatest one--she never got a C, D, or even a B in school. On the other side Angeline was mean, lazy, and hated school. She had a pet snake which was really fat. He ate the neighbor's dog, Sophie! In addition, there was a cat named Flades. He was just like Angeline, except lazier.

Angela was in school. She was one of the 20 students chosen to be part of the Saber Council. At her Saber meeting she had to read the funniest story ever. However, she peeked and saw the girl next to her having the saddest story ever. Then it was Angela's turn to read her story. One thing the Saber Council did was help clean the library. Angela was chosen to be with three girls and one boy. Angela got to clean the table--it was really old.

Then she saw something growing. It was a pencil! Angela said, "Oh it's just a pencil, how lame," but by the time she turned back the pencil was floating. Angela turned to the pencil and saw a weird genie talking.

"This pencil is not an ordinary pencil. You can draw or erase anything, Angela. It's your job to protect Lead Street with Sparky," the genie said.

"That dog who does commercials full of cuteness?" Angela said.

The Genie nodded and said, "Yes, I will pull him for you."

Suddenly, the light turned off then quickly back on, and the dog appeared. The dog said, "Oh, it's you, genie."

The genie smiled and said, "Yeah. Angela, he already knows. I will leave you with the magical pencil. See you never!"

Angela said, "So Sparky, do you, um, like bacon?"

Sparky said, "Um… I'm vegetarian."

Angela smiled and pointed the pencil at him and said, "You will have the head of a dog, the body of a human, and the hands of an octopus."

Sparky was now a Doctopuman. Sparky snatched the pencil away, made her legs into a robot, and gave her the power to turn invisible. They were arguing over who will have the pencil when they accidently threw the pencil out the window and at the same time they both said, "Oops!"

Then, Flades the Cat got the pencil. "Muahaha" Flades said. They all started fighting.

Angela saw Angeline and she said, "Ha! Loser!"

Sparky got his octopus hands and snatched the pencil away, and Angeline quickly threw the pencil at his balloon body and the pencil broke and Flades turned into a cute cat. No longer was Sparky famous. Now it was Flades' turn.

SUPER SEA WOMAN AND SORCERER

BY NATALIE M., GRADE 2

Once upon a time, a brother and sister were inseparable. They lived in Jamaica, but as they got older the brother, Mark, became Lord Dark Water, who was a super villain who wanted to dominate the sea and get rid of all the animals.

DON DON DON!

But his sister, Jamie, became Super Sea Woman, protector of the sea and animals. So if Lord Dark Water tried to do any kind of monkey business, she would know and also see it because if someone was doing something evil she just knew. That was her power, to see everything.

Lord Dark Water's power was shooting leeches out of his hands.

Super Sea Woman didn't want leeches, so she took her job seriously. Because if anyone saw leeches, they would know who's off duty. Lord Dark Water was black and hairless and short. Super Sea Woman is black, tall, and has long, blue hair.

First, Lord Dark Water and Super Sea Woman were in the water and Lord Dark Water was spreading some fake dolphin food so the dolphins would be attracted to it, and Super Sea Woman caught him.

They argued back and forth until 50 dolphins were eating all the food. Then, when Lord Dark Water looked and saw that all of the food was gone, he said "Aw man."

Super Sea Woman said, "Yes!"

But Lord Dark Water still had some of the smell on him, so he smiled and then he said, "I mean, aw rats!" Super Sea Woman smelled the food and saw some dolphins rushing over. She swam out of the way really quickly and when Lord Dark Water saw that the dolphins were rushing, he was shocked!

So the dolphins tricked Lord Dark Water to show him how fun the sea really is, then they finally tired out Lord Dark Water. He said, "Wow this is fun! The dolphins go fast, the whales do flips. This is awesome."

THE SUPERMAN WHO FELL OFF A CLIFF

BY MALACHI M., GRADE 2

One day in the city of Coocooland in a cloud volcano tree, Mr. Ice and Mr. Dice were fighting their enemy, Mr. Octopus.

As they fought Mr. Octopus pushed Mr. Dice off a cliff. He fell off a cliff and got hurt. Mr. Octopus tried to hypnotize Mr. Ice, but it did not work.

Mr. Dice survived. He lived in the ice castle. He wasn't able to work for Mr. Ice. He lost his job.

Mr. Ice and Mr. Octopus got into a fight. Mr. Ice used his freeze breath to turn him into a block of ice.

THE CREATURE

BY SEBASTIAN V., GRADE 3

Once upon a time there was a mystery creature that was as tall as a building and as light as a feather. But when he was walking, he ran into somebody named Mr. Fables that was stranger than Mystery Creature.

Side-note: Mystery Creature's hair is metal and it deflects everything and his brain made up his whole body.

Mr. Fables was in disguise as the Joker, but was actually a superhero. When they teamed up, they fought the real Joker. A lightning bolt struck down and a man appeared. His name was Electro. When they fought Electro, he won the fight, but Mystery Creature and Mr. Fables had another plan to attack Electro.

Their plan was to make a suit out of rubber to put on them. They would need a few thousand pounds of rubber. Anyway, did you know? Rubber is the reason you don't get struck by lightning, that's why they are wearing rubber.

To be continued…

THE PLANT WHERE MY PARENTS DISAPPEARED

BY LEAH B., GRADE 8

There is a girl that would always wear a red cape whenever she would go out with her family and she would wear it to sleep, too! She is one of my neighbors. She has this pet wolf that she calls a dog. My name is Jack and I live in a humongous plant. I have a family of pigs that live down the street and they come visit me every day.

There's this tortoise that always has races with their best friend. "Hare" is his name. We all have one thing in common: we all love playing volleyball everyday after school and work. "We have a game tonight actually," I said to myself.

I have a best friend, his name is Giant. He's been a mother and father figure ever since my mother and father fell off of our last home plant and never returned. We hope they're still alive. The Three Little Pigs are always dropping off food at the bottom of the plant I live in. They drop off food like eggs, bread, ham, and other basic foods because I really can't leave the plant.

Nobody can come up the beanstalk because it is too tall and they heard that my parents fell off of it so nobody else would come up. I'm scared to go down. Giant won't let me go down the beanstalk because of what happened to my mom and dad. He said I'm not ready for the real world. Tonight I will plan to run away while the giant is sleeping and for the first time ever I will do it alone and try my best not to return. Night comes. I go downstairs, walk by the kitchen and see Giant in the kitchen getting a drink of water. I try not to get caught and walk around but Giant sees me trying to get out and he pushes me over the plant's ledge.

To be continued…

PRINCESS WHO?

BY ARIANA B., GRADE 7

In a kingdom far away, lived Me. Yeah, I'm going to tell you my story. I was supposed to get married in a week. And I didn't like that. I mean, my father was like, "Blah blah, married in a week, blah, why can't you be like your cousins?" I am the second son of the Ling family, and we're royalty.

I am 22 years old, and here, I'm stuck in a tower in the middle of nowhere now. I'm not talking a cute little Rapunzel tower; I'm talking about the Great Wall of China type tower. All of a sudden, a tall woman came up to me and said, "I will let you leave under one condition. You will make my family rich and never come back." She stood waiting in front of me for an answer.

"No," I said. "You will marry me, and I will make your family rich."

At the same time, I was thinking, what am I doing?

"What? No," she said.

"Yes, you will, and I will make sure of it." I got off the chair and grabbed her. "Come on, show me your parents." The whole way she didn't say anything.

"Over here," she said. I knew that it was a win-win. I mean, she'll have the money and she will marry a handsome man, too. "Hey...hey you," she said, "what's your name?"

"Oh, mine?...Alex Prince. Prince, for short, though," I said. She stayed quiet for a while, but she told me that I would have to meet her parents.

"Mom, dad, this is my hubby," she said.

"Stop pulling my leg, we all know he is just a stranger you picked off the street."

She laughed.

"No, I am her husband, and I am also rich."

Their jaws dropped.

"Well, my son-in-law, I would love to know you more."

She changed, I grabbed her hand and told her I needed to go back to the castle. She grinned at me. When we were done, I got on my horse and so did she. It took almost an hour to reach the castle and she looked surprised.

"Wow, I never knew how big a castle could be. It seemed so tiny," she mumbled as soon as we entered.

"Pow!" I woke up. The room was dark. At the end of the room, there was a tiny light that brightened up the room.

"Help. . .help!" I screamed.

"Pow!" again. It was a girl's room, full of memories that didn't belong to me. Was it hers? I saw her mom in the memories.

"Hey, umm, when you marry me, I will make you the happiest wife ever," I said. She gave me a sad, happy, relieved type of smirk. As we entered, father looked and her and said, "My prayers have been answered. I can have grandchildren."

"Yeah, so this is...um...what is your name again?" I mumbled.

"Audrey is my name," she said, proudly.

My father said, "Thank you for being with my son. Um...Alex, go and send her to her room."

I don't know if she would want to talk to me, so I didn't. When we arrived, she looked at me with the weirdest face. "This is mine?" she said, confused. I nodded.

Later on, when we were going to have dinner, I asked her to meet up with me at the garden, but I almost waited for an hour. Finally, I heard her. What happened was just what I thought, but she said, "Sorry, I got lost five times."

She sat next to me and we talked about her past. I couldn't believe how harsh her story was! When she was talking I listened to every single word, not letting myself cry. She was so positive on the outside, but when she finished, she shed tears and she hugged me. I felt this weird feeling that made me hug her back.

"Hey, you don't have to marry me, I will still give you money," I said softly.

"No, I am fine. You're the first one who ever listened to me and me feel special."

Sometimes you have to listen to the words people have to say not everything has a perfect ending or background. Stop and listen to people and be their guide.

THE STORY OF THE GORILLA

BY JULIAN Q., GRADE 6

Once upon a time, a gorilla was walking. Then he met this girl and one day they got mad at each other and he lifted a house and under the house there were pipes, and in the pipes there was a lot of stuff and that stuff was flying around like leaves on a windy day.

And that's how he discovered his powers.

He used his powers to make a living. Someone asked him to lift their house for them. He used it to move their house to a different state (or something like that). They were arguing about couple problems. They live in a world full of gorillas called Gorilla Land. When they got mad and he lifted a house, he threw it across the WORLD.

RAINBOW'S ADVENTURE

BY VALERY V., GRADE 3

One day a unicorn named Rainbow was in Guatemala. She discovered that she had powers.

She said, "I wish I was a bat," and she turned into one. "Yay, I am a bat and I am free," she shouted. Then she went to the cave. She remembered that she was scared of caves, so she turned back and said, "I change my mind." So she turned back into a unicorn.

She did not like being a bat because the cave was dark and crowded. So after she went back to being a unicorn, she went to the fairy flower garden, where all the shapeshifting unicorns lived. That's where she learned how to use her shapeshifting abilities.

After Rainbow learned how to control her powers, she went back home and showed her mom and dad what she could do. They were so proud of her and they wanted to give Rainbow a surprise because she now knew how to use her powers and she could train at the Fairy Flower Garden if there was a predator coming for her.

DRAGON QUEST

BY KRISTUPAS R., GRADE 6

Once upon there was a dragon who sat on dollar bills. He lived in a school bank. Then a penguin came to visit the dragon. The penguin asked, "Is it comfy?"

He said the dollar bills were rough. The dragon left to get something to eat. The baby dragon came to eat something and the penguin went to the pound.

The penguin asked what kind of gold to get. The dragon said to go to Mount Dearmmor. The penguin set off on his journey. Then the penguin went to meet the dark dragon with specks of metal and a fire breath.

INVISIBLE BOY

BY CARLOS P., GRADE 6

One day there was a person named Carlos. He was lazy all the time, and he was invisible—no one can see him. Carlos's brother Caesar was always so mean, and they were enemies. Carlos used to be seen, but one day, Carlos's brother kidnapped Carlos while he was sleeping and turned him invisible. Carlos's brother was jealous because Carlos had a lot of friends, and Caesar had no friends. Caesar was always getting bullied.

Carlos's brother bought the potion at a garage sale. Carlos planned to get revenge by scaring all his enemies. After getting tired he always slept a lot. After days passed by, Caesar finally got the potion, so he was going to use it on Carlos. Caesar realized that he was sleeping, so Caesar said to himself, "it's the perfect chance!" Caesar drank the potion, and his stomach felt so bad he was freaking out. He realized the potion was in a bottle that turned atoms tiny.

To be continued...

CANDY LAND

BY SIPHO F., GRADE 5

Candy Land is a great planet far, far, away from Earth. Sipho goes to Burr School. Sipho has curly hair and wears a Packers jersey (which is all green for their home jersey while the Bears home jersey is orange and blue). His sidekick is a chameleon named Jeff.

Their antagonist is Camel, a big Bears follower who wants Sipho to like the Bears, while Sipho wants Camel to like the Packers. When the Bears lose, and the Packers win, Sipho brags. And when the Packers lose and the Bears win, Camel boasts. They always boast about which team wins. The big problem is that Sipho and Camel argue about which team is better; they are not yelling, but it is still arguing.

One day Camel goes to Sipho's house. The house is a Packers symbol made out of a cookie. It smells like a chocolate chip cookie, feels smooth, and if you hit it crumbs will fall down. Camel does not go Sipho's house at all--he's just going because the Packers and the Bears are playing each other.

The game starts and the Bears kicks off and the Packers run the ball and the player runs with his little gingerbread legs all the way into the end zone. Sipho starts going crazy! He's so happy.

The Packers keep scoring! And Sipho keeps doing these crazy celebrations while Camel is resistant to look at Sipho's celebrations. Sipho's celebrations are very precise. He does Irish dance moves for about 30 seconds, yelling and spinning a ball and running around the ball. And Sipho hangs Jeff on the roof and shines a light on him and Jeff changes colors, so Jeff is like a disco ball for Sipho's dance moves.

At the end of the game, the Packers win and Camel is so frustrated that he ends up liking the Packers. Sipho thought to himself: "Mission accomplished."

JEFF VS. SHADOW

BY DIEGO M., GRADE 3

One day, Jeff and Shadow and his sidekick, Paper Cut, who is cool for no reason, were arguing about who was stronger. Without saying anything, Papercut shot paper stairs from his blaster. Then Jeff used his fire sword and slashed 15 times, then Papercut was weak. He had only 55,559,951 lives. But Shadow came along. He had 99,999,999,998 lives while Jeff had 99,999,999,999, so Shadow was weaker.

Anyways, while Jeff was thinking, Shadow used his Dark Fire Breath that does 9,555,599,999 knock back, but it did no good. Jeff had 9.904×10^{10} lives, so Jeff's fire sword to the max did 99,999,999 knock back so Shadow had 9.999×10^{10} lives. Then Papercut to the rescue. He used infinity paper bombs. It did 99,999,999 drawback. Jeff had 9.034×10^{10} lives. So Shadow finished him with a flaming fire beam that does 999,999,999,999 knock back. Shadow made Jeff have -9.9097×10^{10} lives, so Jeff made a fire lighting beam that did a lot of damage. Shadow had 5,555 lives left, so Shadow, a legendary force, did more. Jeff had 1×10^{10} lives left. Shadow did a fire beam and made 5,559,999,999. Jeff had 3000 lives.

Jeff gave up in rage and was mad, so since Shadow and Papercut won the Battle, he hated them ever since that day.

THE GIRL

BY JARITZA M., GRADE 8

There was a girl named Amanda. She was thirteen, and she used to go to school. No one liked her. They used to push her and be rude and throw her things and everyone used to make fun of her.

Amanda was upset, so she talked to her dog. Her dog was her best friend (and her only friend). She told her dog, named Mia, "I'm over this. I'm tired of everyone making fun of me, and I won't let this happen again."

The next day, the same things happened, and she said, "stop!" Amanda saw the girl that was being rude to her and noticed that she had been through a lot. She saw that she didn't have a good life, and the girl was going through a lot. Amanda noticed that she could go into the other girl's life and change things around, and even though the girl was rude to her, Amanda felt bad so she changed her life and made her a nice person. She found out that her dog was there to guide her to be a good person and not to use her powers for bad, so after all that, she decided to help people.

THE SWORD OF SUMMER

BY CHANIEL K., GRADE 5

One day in Candy Land, Nibor was doing his typical thing: robbing a bank.

And he had a awesome plan. He wanted to take the Sword of Summer, which can cut through anything and turn it into caramel.

But first he had to go through the impenetrable vault of Candy Land, which is made of jawbreakers.

While he was getting the Sword of Summer, he saw Super Daniel. Nibor was afraid of Super Daniel because he had the power of strength and flight, and all Nibor had was the power of intelligence. So he had to keep low.

Before he took the Sword of Summer, he had to find the code, so he went to the smartest guy he knew, Chaniel. Chaniel is the smartest dude in the universe and he loves alchemy.

Nibor went to Chaniel, and Chaniel gave him the code. It was 2905888—the code to everything in the universe. So after Nibor got the code, he walked all the way to the impenetrable vault and he saw a penny in it. Somebody had already stolen everything!

Nibor was depressed, and he thought about that moment for the rest of his life.

ROBLOX, ROB-LOX, ROBLOX

BY COURTNEY M., GRADE 6

The conflict between Natalie 1 and Natalie 2 is that they both love roblox and want to play, but they don't know who's going to play first.

So since they don't know who's going first… they… decide… TO HAVE A WAR!

THE ROBLOX WAR!

So they get all their friends and all their stuffed animals so they can throw them at each other's team, and whichever teams knocks the other team out first gets to play first.

Natalie 1's team has 20 people. Natalie 2's team has 25 people. Before the war, Natalie 1 gives a tiny speech. She says, "Guys, we can do this. We can beat them, and if we don't win, just know that it's not your fault and that you tried your best."

The team responds, "YEAH WE GOT THIS!" So the teams prepare for war. Now, the question we've all been asking… WHO WILL WIN THE WAR?!

Fast forward: So it appears that nobody won the war.

THE PIG BROTHERS AND FARMER AX

BY JOSUE S., GRADE 5

In a big red barn that smelled like hay, cows and sheep were starving. Even the pigs were starving! You might think pigs are hoggers of food, but these pigs were different. Oinky, Wilbur, and Saveal were heroes but they just didn't know it. Oinky was fast, strong, and the biggest. Wilbur was smart and loved pranks. Saveal was weak and picky about his food. The trio were orphans and lived in Farmer Ax's barn.

Then one day while they were looking for food, the door slammed open.

"Woah!" Farmer Ax walked in and said, "Come here, Oinky!"

Oinky ran away as fast as he could, but he crashed into the fence and got caught. Wilbur and Saveal ran to save him, but it was too late. Oinky was taken to the place they all feared: the kitchen.

Wilbur and Saveal were very weak, but they had to save their brother. Farmer Ax left the door open, so they sneaked into the kitchen and saw Oinky in the cage. They saw Farmer Ax get his knife ready.

Then Saveal made the loudest sound on Earth. The farmer covered his ears and let go of Oinky. They all pushed the Farmer in the stove and cooked him.

On Christmas Day the pigs invited all the animals to feast and they all ate the farmer. Then they lifted their cups of water and said, "To the pigs!"

The End

THE SISTER

BY ASHA H., GRADE 8

Hello, my name is Spike. I live underground on the south coast of Jamaica. I live with my father. I have never met my mother. I have killed exactly 110 bugs. I've always wanted a sibling but never got one.

But anyway, here's my story. I am sixteen years old and I like to wreak havoc on my world. The country of Jamaica is a nice place but not when it is destroyed.

This hero, Rose, who I hate so much, always ruins my plans for world domination. But I always end up winning our battles.

My father and I were together and I just so happened to see her. We saw each other from afar. My father looked at her and said "Rose, you've grown so much." I looked at my dad and he said that she, my worst enemy, is my twin sister. She started to explain that our mother is dead. So as my father and Rose were talking I just started to run and I kept running and running and didn't stop.

1908

BY JULIAN V., GRADE 7

Once upon a time there was a kid named Tony. He always played baseball. He wanted to play in the MLB.

His dad told him,"You should play basketball," because his dad played in the NBA.

Tony still went to play baseball. "I will be second base or shortstop." Everyone laughed.

"This is basketball, kid!" they said.

He didn't know how to play and he was too short. He was like 4-foot-4. He gave up. He told them, "Come play me in baseball." His dad got really mad. He told his dad, "Just watch, Dad."

Next week in Chicago, he went to a Cubs game. The Cubs stadium smelled like hotdogs and popcorn. He caught Javy Báez's ball. He was really happy.

Later, the kids from basketball joined. They all scrimaged. He hit five home runs in one inning. He was really happy. The basketball kids were super mad. They stopped playing. He cracked up.

Ten years later, he got drafted to play in the MLB for the Cubs and played with his favorite player: Javy Báez. He told his dad, "Told you I would make it!"

SEEING ABRAHAM LINCOLN

BY KAREN V., GRADE 4

Samantha's mom passed away. She went to visit her mom's grave. But she stopped at the store to buy roses and daisies, because her mom liked them very much. Samantha and her mom liked to plant flowers together in the garden. They didn't have flowers there, so she want to a greenhouse.

Samantha met the woman who owned the store, Tabitha. She wore a long dress with daisies, and this reminded Samantha of her mother who wore the same dress. Samantha felt happy because she was near her mother again, but sad because she had passed away. She wore that the dress when they went to Giovanni's, to eat her favorite dish, spaghetti.

Samantha picked the flowers, complimented Tabitha on the dress, and went to the graveyard with her dad and her sisters, Ruth and Natasha. Their dad wore a blue sweater and a gray shirt. Samantha's sisters wore purple and neon green dresses.

They put the flowers onto the grave. Everyone was really sad. Samantha went to the car and found Lincoln's grave. Samantha started to cry loudly. So loudly, it woke up Abraham Lincoln. He woke up and followed her. Lincoln was sitting next to Samantha's dad in the front seat, but her dad didn't know.

When they got home, Samantha went to her room and found Lincoln on her bed. She got scared at first because she didn't know who he was.

Then, Abraham Lincoln introduced himself, "Hi, I'm Abraham Lincoln, and I'm sorry if I scared you."

Samantha said, "It's O.K. I'm glad it's you."

Lincoln said, "Your mother is a really fun woman."

Samantha said "Mom played hide-and-seek with me in the house. Mom used to plant flowers with me in the garden. I once tried to say hello underwater, and accidently drank some water."

Lincoln laughed hard.

THE END

DISRESPECT

BY ABIGAIL M., GRADE 8

Lots of middle-aged people are in an OK-sized building that is referred to as a laundromat. My stuff was on a folding table, and I had taken the laundry out of the dryer, which is on the right, and put some on a table. I scattered them because I don't like my clothing being in a pile.

Later, a short, medium-skin-tone old lady decided she owned someone. She moved my stuff, but before this, she asked in a rude way, "Can you move your stuff?" And then she didn't even give me enough time to say anything, but took it upon herself to move my stuff.

The next week, she was saying to my brother that he was in her way. He didn't like the comment. A customer got involved and said, "You should be an example and respect everyone, regardless of age." She tried to fight it, but her husband said, "It's not worth it, let's go." They left and everyone clapped in happiness and pride.

THE BRAIN FIGHT

BY JULIAN P., GRADE 3

One day in sandy sands, Chomfer and Zomboss were fighting. It wasn't fair because Chomfer was taller than Zomboss. But Zomboss was as mad as my mom when my brother doesn't do his homework. He was so mad, he cracked his head open! Nothing came out because Zomboss has no brain.

It was very dusty and they used shoes and mud because Chomfer and Zomboss were mad. Chomfer was a plant with spikes on his head, and he had a big mouth. Zomboss had wrinkles on his head because he was so smart. Chomfer was trying to stop Zomboss from eating Crazy Dave's brain.

"Give me that!" Zomboss said.

"Never!" Chomfer said.

"How about we make a deal?" Chomfer said. "I will go get you a brain!"

He found one. He gave it to Zomboss. Yay, he saved the day! And the land went back to normal.

FIGHT AT WORK

BY BRANDON A., GRADE 6

One day, the alarm started Fernando's day. He woke up, took a shower, ate breakfast, and got dressed for work. Fernando wanted to be in the Army so he could serve and fight for his country. But his family didn't want him to, so Fernando worked and studied so he could work in a office. He went to work with his stuff and it was his first day. It was everyone in the office's first day too. It was awkward for the first week but everyone started getting along.

Five months passed. More people started working at the office and the boss went for a road trip with his wife. After a few days passed, one of Fernando's coworkers, Mac, saw a website for a Rolls Royce dealership. He tapped on the site and started reading 'bout it. Mac signed on to work at the job.

Three days later!

After Mac started working, he saw that there were some cookies in the front of the office for free along with milk and hot cocoa, so he went and got some and liked it. Every day he gets cookies and milk. One time, Fernando and Mac went to get cookies at the same time and Fernando grabbed half of the cookie but Mac grabbed like 1/4 of the cookie (it's weird how the story went to jobs then food, then math, like come on). After the cookie, Mac got mad and started a little fight.

There was a substitute for the the boss until the real boss came back from the road trip with his wife. The boss came inside the building when he was done taking out the trash because the janitor was late. The boss wanted to help the janitor work a little bit, so he took out the trash, just to be nice and give her a few hours too. The boss came in and stopped the little fight. "Why are you guys fighting?" asked the boss.

Mac said, "What? Who are you?"

"I'm your boss, Mike. I'm working here until Daniel comes back!" said Mike.

Mac: "Oh okay, I thought you worked here, but it was your first day."

Mike: "Nah, I'm your boss from now until Daniel gets back from his road trip!"

Fernando: "So you're just going to talk about you instead of gettin mad?!"

Mike: "Oh yeah, I jus' forgot what you jus' said. Hehehe, ay, guess what?"

At the same time, Fernando and Mac said, "What?"

Mike: "Chicken butt, hahahhahahahaha!"

Fernando: "Really? Chicken butt? Yeah that's really funny, hehehehe."

Mac: "Oh my god, bro, really, you know what, Imma jus' go back and work on stuff."

Fernando: "Yeah, same."

Mike: "Okay, good, Imma go use the bathroom."

After work Fernando went back home and saw that the lights were off.
Fernando: "Honey, I'm back, hellooo, hellooo!"
Fernando went to his room and on the door there was a note that said,

Hey, baby, sorry if I'm not home, I went shopping for the tool I need to fix the shower, 'ight, sry, love you from Jazmine.

Fernando was happy for the note because he got to hear from his girlfriend. He took off his shoes and changed into shorts and a plain black shirt. Then he went to sleep until Jazmine came back home.
After thirty minutes Jazmine came back. She set down the food and the shirts that she bought.
Jazmine: "I'm back, teddy bear!"
Fernando: "Hey, teddy bear!" (They called each other 'teddy bear' because Fernando was hairy and Jazmine was too, but from her arms, like how some women have hairy arms, too. So they call each other 'teddy bear'.)

The next day, Fernando went back to work and he saw Mac wearing some black jeans under his butt, jus' like how in the hoodie does it. It was weird that someone like that puts their pants down in a good place and fancy too. Mac was really, really mad at Fernando because of yesterday.
Mac: "Ay, Fernando watch me take your cookie, 'ight!"
Fernando: "Why, we just came at the same time,

Mac. Chill, I can give you homemade cookies, bro!"

Mac: "Ay, don't call me your bro because I ain't your bro!"

Fernando: "'Ight, 'ight, sorry, Mac!"

Mac: "Better!"

After work, Mac went back home where there is a hood. He got back and changed into his Gucci shirt and his Gucci sweater. Every time you see Mac, you will always see him in a hoodie. Mostly everybody in the hood calls him Hoodie, because he likes hoodies and wears one 24/7.

After that, he went to the gang and hung out every Saturday, that's how Mac lives his life. Mac is very, very unhealthy because he really does stuff that could kill him but it's his life.

The next day, Mac didn't go to work. Instead, he went to hang out in the streets with friends because everyone saw his story on an app called Snapchat and Instagram. Mac had been stopped by the cops before and had been in trouble like five times already. Mac didn't like Fernando just because of the cookie he didn't get. Mac didn't go to work the rest of the week and the next week, he went back ready to fight Fernando. After work, Mac pretended to leave to go back home, but he came back and waited for Fernando so he could follow Fernando into his house. Five minutes later, Fernando came out from the office, got in his car, and left. When Mac saw Fernando leave, he followed him just to see what he does so Mac could ruin it (just sayin' Mac is weird).

Mac left a note for Fernando on his front door and rang the bell. When Fernando heard it, his wife opened it and read it. After reading it, she showed Fernando the note and she started to cry.

Jazmine: "What's this? I don't wanna get taken by someone, baby, please get help! Wait, what did you do to make him or her mad?"

Fernando looked at her like *Whattt?* He asked, "What do you mean, honey? Why are you crying?"

Jazmine: "Here, read this." Jazmine gave the note to Fernando so he could read why she was crying. He read the note out loud.

Fernando: "Whoever is reading this, ur wife or husband is going to be gone if you keep messing around wit' me, 'ight."

Jazmine: "See, what did I tell you, I'm saying tha-"
Fernando cut Jazmine off.

Fernando: "-that I'm having problems at work, and yes, yes I am, wit' this guy named Mac."

Jazmine: "Last name?"

Fernando: "Davidson."

Jazmine: "Oh, no, I...I gotta go, I'm sorry, but I have had problems with him, too, honey. Let's move somewhere else far from him!"

Fernando: "Did he do something to you, like very bad, 'cause I don't like when other people mess with my teddy bear!"

Jazmine: "No, you gotta stay here with me. I don't want you to get hurt, okay!"

Fernando ignored Jazmine and changed, then walked outside ready to fight Hoodie because he could see where he was (Mac was dumb because he left his headlights on). Fernando knew what kind of car he had.

Mac got out the car and said, "Who you lookin at, huh, huh huh? Tell me who you lookin' at!"

Fernando: "Why you say stuff about my wife and me? That we are going to be gone, huh? You tell me why.

Is it because of the dumb cookie?!"

Mac: "No, you were makin' fun of me."

Fernando: "When? I respect people, I don't hurt people."

Mac: "Well, you did hurt me." Mac walked up closer to get ready while Jazmine looked out the window. She rushed to the door and yelled.

Jazmine: "No, Fernando, don't!" Jazmine went inside to call Brandon, one of Fernando's best friends since third grade.

Jazmine: "Hello, Brandon, are you there? Please answer!"

Brandon: "Yeah, yeah, I'm here. What happened? You sound scared."

Jazmine: "Fernando is going to fight with this guy named Mac."

Brandon: "On my way, Jazmine."

Jazmine: "Okay!"

Brandon: "Just stay calm, stay on the li..."

Jazmine ended the call.

Brandon went to his car and drove to Fernando's house. Six minutes later, Brandon arrived and saw Fernando yelling at Mac about stuff he doesn't know about and about life and that was rough, too. Brandon got out of the car and saw another guy in Mac's car. Brandon looked back at Mac and they started to fight. They punched each other and the other person got out of the car and Brandon ran to the guy and headlocked him while Fernando handled Mac.

I was looking at Fernando. The only thing I saw was Fernando throw a heavy, strong punch that knocked out Mac and made him forget about everything. I let the other person go and he ran away with Mac.

To be continued...

THE BUDDY
BY JOSEPH B., GRADE 3

One morning, in the Dark Woods, there was a big wolf and a mouse. The wolf was going to eat the mouse. The mouse said, "Don't eat me! You need three wishes to eat me. I am a little mouse. You need to respect me."

So the wolf wished for a house, a chicken, and a bird. He wanted those animals because he did not want to eat big animals like a lion, a bear, or an eagle. He was so hungry but the big animals were hard to catch. The small animals were easy to catch for the wolf. The wolf still wanted to eat the mouse but it was hard.

The mouse stopped running because he was tired. The wolf came and he said, "I'm going to eat you!"

The mouse ran away. The wolf said, "Where are my three wishes!?" The mouse slipped in a pond. He kept running. The wolf was chasing him but it was too late.

He was so angry because he needed to run faster.

The mouse was in his house. The wolf knocked the door down but then three mice came and the one mouse went to the little house, and the other mouse went to the medium house, and the third mouse went to the large house. The wolf huffed and puffed the small house so the mouse ran to the medium house. Then he huffed and puffed the medium house so the two mice ran to the large house. He huffed and puffed the big house but he couldn't destroy it so the three mice were safe.

And the wolf ran away.

JEFF THE BUFF TURTLE

BY DIEGO R., GRADE 7

One day, Bob the Evil Snake thought it would be cool if he bombed Diego with Taco Bombs. So Bob built an evil flying taco truck and flew over DiegoLand. He started to drop the bombs but they were magnetic so they came back to his truck and blew him up. He had to go back to his lair and fix the truck.

Meanwhile, Jeff the Buff Turtle went to go see what Bob was doing because Jeff the Buff Turtle knew Bob was always up to something. When Jeff walked in, he found Bob fixing the taco bomber. Jeff tried to stop Bob but he got away! Jeff couldn't fly and the bombs were falling already! Jeff used his nine pack (which is his abs) to fling him over to Bob. He got into the truck and punched Bob with his face! Bob the snake knew he was going to be caught so he tried to talk his way out of it but Jeff punched him with his nine pack. Jeff took Bob to jail again and Jeff ate a taco bomb but he has a very strong stomach and the explosion didn't affect him.

The End

IRIS VS. PROFESSOR BLAH BLAH

BY MAYRA C., GRADE 4

One day on Pluto, on a Frozen Lake Day where everyone goes to the frozen lake to eat soup all day, Iris goes home to eat pizza and watch Netflix. She texts the pizza place on her phone.

Then they call her to say that her pizza order is ready and they ask her if she wants delivery or pickup. She always says delivery and her pizza was there in thirty minutes. The man that delivers the pizza is mean and says she is ugly.

The man's name is Professor Blah Blah. He was planning to retire after ruling the world and having a lifetime's supply of Big Macs. Owning 500,000 Burger Kings means getting to read all of the essays of seniors in high school and college students, and giving a two-day school schedule for everyone in preschool to 8th grade.

To be continued . . .

SECRET SUPERHEROES

BY ALONDRA M., GRADE 4

One day, there was a secret superhero named Olivia. Her superhero name was Crystal. She had a sidekick named Emma who went to the same high school. Her superhero name was Flame. There was another girl who went to the same high school as Emma and Olivia but was a bad person. Her name was Ivy. Her real name was Andrea. She pretended to be nice to Olivia and Emma at school…

Until there was a problem caused by Andrea.

Olivia, Emma, and Andrea were using their powers with the whole school watching them. Now, the whole school knew that two superhero girls were fighting one villain. Crystal's powers were a crystal shield, flying, and teal hair. She wore a teal shirt, teal shoes, and blue jeans. Flame had red hair. She wore a red skirt and a blue shirt. Ivy wore a green dress and had neon green hair. Crystal was using her powers, but she couldn't because Ivy used her powers to tie her up with plants growing out of the floor. Flame came and made Ivy and the whole school laugh and Ivy was laughing so hard that she couldn't hold Crystal with her powers.

Finally, they defeated Ivy and went back to their normal life. Well, almost normal. Every day at school people have been asking, begging, and bugging Olivia and Emma for their secrets.

A SHARK IN GRANNY'S HOUSE

BY ADOLFO T., GRADE 3

The shark was driving in his peach car when, suddenly, the gasoline ran out. He looked around and saw Granny's house and the neighbor's house. The shark decided to go to Granny's house, because he thought Granny's house was safer, but it was not.

The shark went into the house and went upstairs to look for food. He saw the meat in the toilet, then he went upstairs and he dropped in the door. He hid so Granny couldn't see him and this house is underwater and he found the pliers and he lost the boards and he drove the board and pot into the broken spot and he drove the hammer and broke the camera and he grabbed the pliers and he cut the three blue strings and he found the melon and he chopped it off and found the blue key.

The shark opened the lock and he only needed the master key and he found the screwdriver and he took off a screw and he found the weapons keys and he used the code and found lasers and he thought, Granny, and he shot the master lock and he was safe. He didn't know where to go.

THE CAR

BY EZEKIEL M., GRADE 6

Once upon a time in Chicago, there was a quarterback nicknamed "The Car" because he was big and he could hit other players hard. He had a dog named QB Junior and he was the mascot of the team because he could run for a long time.

One day, a game was about to start. Some baseball players arrived with a big sign that said "Football is bad and baseball is good." The dog smelled them coming and got mad.

The game started and, as soon as The Car was going to throw the football, the baseball players started booing. One of them hit someone and they had an argument.

The Car said, "We can have the field on Monday and Wednesday, you can have the field on Tuesday and Saturday." The baseball players agreed with the football player. They were friends and they cheered for each other.

JURASSIC ISLAND

BY JULIAN D., GRADE 8

In Antartica, people were searching for something. They found a mammoth trapped in ice. They used power tools to break it open. Then after that, a helicopter came to ship it to Mexico.

Jurassic Island is a place where dinosaurs feel safe after the dinosaurs escaped Jurassic World in 2015 and the volcano eruption in 2018. WELCOME TO JURASSIC ISLAND.

They had everything like an ice age exhibit, a restaurant, McDonald's, Uncle Julio's, gift shops, museum, rides, fun activities, and more.

One week after the dinosaurs arrived, a flood reached Jurassic Island and the control room and the circuit breaker room's power got shut down.

Even the electric bars that kept the dangerous dinosaurs secure went off. Every security system was off except for the raptors' cage because they had their own power. They live in the mountains and their cage is made from barred metal. The first one to break out was the Dilophasaurus. The Compey broke out next and finally, the T.Rex. After the dinosaurs broke out in 2034, the scientists worried that creating dinosaurs who will break out and want to break others out will affect the Earth.

SOPHIA AND HER STEP-GRANDMA

BY VANESSA T., GRADE 5

Once upon a time, there was a girl named Sophia. Her dream was to go inside a castle. She lived with her grandma, who was actually her step-grandma. Her grandma wouldn't let her do anything. The only thing Sophia could do was clean and she hated to clean. While she cleaned, she thought about the castle she lived close to.

One day, the people who worked at the castle gave out invitations for a ball. Sophia wanted to go but she didn't have an invitation, although her step-grandma got one. Sophia was sad. She wanted to go.

The day of the ball, Sophia's step-grandma made her clean and told her if she didn't, she would be kicked out of the house. When Sophia was done, she took a walk around the castle. Her step-grandma spotted her from inside the ball. She went outside and started yelling at Sophia, who just stood there, still. One minute later, the prince went out and ordered the yelling step-grandma to go to jail.

Since Sophia did not have an invitation to the ball, she had no choice but to go home. But then the prince invited her, so she accepted!

The prince asked, "Where are you from?"

Sophia said, "I'm from here. Where are you from?"

"I'm from Chicago and I live here," said the prince.

"Where are your parents?" asked Sophia.

The prince said "They're in Chicago."

"Oh," said Sophia.

When it got dark, she went home. She went to bed thinking her dream had come true.

THE BIG CATCH

BY ISAIAS D., GRADE 7

Once upon a time, there was a green guy named Greeny. Greeny's superpower was to control all animals. His favorite partner was the ant. Greeny's ant could grow from super small to super big.

Greeny and ant sometimes try to save the world. There is this one bad guy named Mr. Genius. He always tries to summon and explode and steal things. But luckily, Greeny and ant are always there to save the day.

Mr. Genius is a weird guy. He was skinny and tall with a big head and purple skin.

Greeny and ant can't catch Mr. Genius because every time they tried, Greeny's sidekick turned into a big ant and he would always knock Greeny over.

Greeny got so mad because his ant had been do-ing that for the past ten missions. When Greeny calmed down, he said, "it's O.K." and he came up with a good plan: Greeny would take Mr. Genius from the front and the ant would take him from the back.

Finally, the bad guy alarm went off! Greeny and the ant raced to the crime scene. It was Mr. Genius rob-bing a bank! When Mr. Genius saw Greeny, Greeny ran and punched him, and they started a punch fight. The ant snuck up behind Mr. Genius and he didn't even know. The ant turned big and caught Mr. Genius and they fi-nally won. Ant and Greeny went home very happy and celebrated.

The End

THE QUEST FOR LEGENDARY POKÉMON

BY CRISTIAN C., GRADE 4

One day in the jungle, Rayquaza wanted to catch all of the legendary Pokémon with his partner Mewtwo. They went up to the sky to find legendaries. There are thirty legendaries in the world and they wanted to find the flying ones first.

Someone else wanted to catch all of the legendary Pokémon. His name was Shadow Lugia. Also, Mewtwo and Rayquaza almost forgot that they both wanted to catch some shiny Pokémon in the world.

Rayquaza and Mewtwo both have a Keystone, which is a tool for Mega-evolution.

Then they heard the legendaries behind them and realized they had been there the whole time. Rayquaza and Mewtwo caught all thirty legendaries at once.

The End

SIDEKICKS MATTER

BY KEONTAE M., GRADE 7

Superman was fighting crime by himself without Supergirl, who was home watching TV. But when Superman got caught, he needed help. Supergirl could feel there was something wrong with Superman so she went to see if Superman was okay.

When Supergirl arrived to help Superman, she saw Killer Croc chain Superman up with Kryptonite to weaken Superman's powers. Supergirl used her heat vision to break the chains and blow up the Kryptonite so Superman could get his powers back. Now Supergirl and Superman could fight Killer Croc. Superman used his heat vision, same as Supergirl. Killer Croc was covered in fire. Superman used his super strength to throw Killer Croc in the water to cool him off and they called the police.

As Killer Croc got arrested, Superman and Supergirl were interviewed.

"Superman, how did you take down Killer Croc?" asked the interviewer.

"I didn't just take down Killer Croc by myself," said Superman. Superman talked about the fight he and Supergirl were in.

"Wow," said the interviewer. As the interview ended, Superman and Supergirl flew into the sky and headed home.

"Finally I can help," said Supergirl.

"What do you mean, Supergirl?" asked Superman.

"I never got to help you fight crime until today."

"I didn't know you felt like that, Supergirl," said Superman. "I'll make it up to you. From now on, you can come fight crime with me."

"Thank you Superman," said Supergirl

"You're welcome," said Superman. After Superman and Supergirl hugged, they never went into another battle by themselves again.

SUNSET VALLEY

BY MICHELLE K., GRADE 5

Once upon a time, three little girls were thrown into an orphanage for mutants. They grew up to be wonderful, capable girls (well, only two of them). Esmerelda and Zebreena were awesome, but McKenzie wasn't really.

Esmerelda had a big poofy afro, pink lips, and dark eyelashes. She wore jeans and galaxy t-shirts, and sometimes her favorite grey sweater. She loved to draw and sadly lost her voice. Her mutant power was a mental power (which is really a lot of powers). Her dog, Flash, is a white, small, scruffy bundle of joy. Zebreena, Esmerelda's best friend, had black, long braids and was a caramel color. She mostly wore white shirts and overalls. She could control minds. She was funny, nice, and optimistic.

She loved to draw with her best friend.

McKenzie, well, let's just say she's something. She's the biggest bully in the orphanage and has blonde hair with brown streaks. She wears skirts and belly shirts. McKenzie was fifteen and she didn't like Esmerelda and Zebreena because they stood up to her.

The girls lived in an orphanage called Sunset Valley. It had a big hill behind it and the hill had roses that smelled awesome. It had a nice staircase to the top. The top of the hill had easels for all the orphans and had a perfect view for drawing.

In Texas, they didn't allow mutants because of one mutant who damaged the city. Zebra (Zebreena) and Essie (Esmerelda) would never do that. But McKenzie probably would.

During class, Essie was bored so she read the Headmistress' mind to see what she was doing. The Headmistress was thinking, *Maybe I'll give the orphans a day off.* When Essie heard this, she slammed her fist on the table for joy. Everybody looked at her weirdly. She said in sign language, "Sorry." Then she told Zebra telepathically what happened. Zebreena smiled and said in her mind, *Maybe we can go on the hill to draw.*

Essie nodded then remembered she had cleaning duty so she couldn't do it. When class finished, she said, in sign language, "I can't do it, I have cleaning duty." Zebreena was bummed, but then she had the idea to draw something for Essie. Zebreena went to the hill and started to draw.

Zebreena was drawing on one of the easels on the hill behind Sunset Valley Orphanage. She was drawing the sunset and she was going to give it to Esmerelda. McKenzie went to bother Zebreena.

"Oh, hi, Zebreena, I didn't know you were here," she said, in a very snotty voice. Zebreena rolled her eyes and tried to get past McKenzie, but McKenzie blocked her.

"Hi, I don't mean to be rude, but you're in my way," Zebreena said.

McKenzie said sarcastically, "Oh, I didn't notice."

Zebreena was being patient, but now she was getting annoyed. "Move," she said. "I don't have time for you."

McKenzie was so surprised by that, she blushed and said, "Um, excuse me, who do you think you are talking to?"

Zebreena was steaming now. She controlled McKenzie and made her move and sit down on dog poop. Zebreena was satisfied and went along to tell Esmerelda the story. When Esmerelda heard the story she laughed really hard until her insides hurt.

Emserelda and Zebra were in their dorm. It was a medium-sized room with turquoise colored walls. There was one black bed and one blue bed with fish on it. Essie's was the blue one, and Zebra's was black. It was 1 p.m., past lunch, when suddenly the intercom said, "All students, please come out of the dorms for a surprise." Everybody came out. An ice cream truck pulled up.

Esmerelda sensed something was wrong. It was the ice cream Zebreena and McKenzie were about to eat. She stopped them and told them there was something wrong with it. Before she could save anybody else, they all took a bite of the horrible ice cream, then everything stopped.

Everybody dropped the ice cream, their eyes went white, and the Headmistress turned into the evil mutant who had destroyed the city, Miss Hypno. She planned to turn all mutants bad, but didn't expect Essie and her friends to not eat the ice cream. She bellowed, "I will not let you foil my plan."

She sent them to a place of mysteries and riddles.

How will these three mutants get out and save the world… Find out in Sunset Valley 2.

ACKNOWLEDGMENTS

We are incredibly grateful for the generosity of our donors, who fund our programs and publications. Thank you for giving our students the opportunity to become published authors and share their stories with the world. You support them in creatively engaging with their community, enriching the lives of their families, teachers, and peers throughout our city. This book was made possible thanks to contributions from the Chauncey and Marion D. McCormick Family Foundation, The Donley Foundation, the James P. and Brenda S. Grusecki Family Foundation, the Judy Family Foundation, the Stanley McNeil Foundation, Christine and Thomas Quinn, Justine Jentes and Dan Kuruna, and Diane Quinn.

To the volunteer tutors who generously dedicate their weekday afternoons to working with this group of bright and curious young authors, we offer a colossal chorus of applause. We feel incredibly lucky to count you among the 826CHI family and are grateful for all you do.

Thank you so much to Grace Molteni, whose lush illustrations created a new world on this cover and illuminated the writing inside. Thank you to our diligent copyeditors, Hailey Dezort, Grant Fuller, Grace Guibert, and Monika Lagaard for making sure our students' work is flawless and ready for publication.

We also extend our eternal gratitude to our fall 2018 interns, who work tirelessly to make everything we do so much better. To Reese Alexander, Monet Foster, Taylor Fustin, Emily Lien, and Julia Pappageorge: thank you.

ABOUT 826CHI

826CHI ("eight-two-six Chicago") is a nonprofit organization dedicated to supporting students ages six to 18 with their creative and expository writing skills, and to helping teachers inspire their students to write. Our services are structured around the understanding that great leaps in learning can happen with individualized attention, and that strong writing skills are fundamental to future success.

With this in mind, we provide after-school tutoring, creative writing workshops, in-school residencies, field trips, support for English Language Learners, and publishing opportunities for Chicago youth—all at absolutely no cost to Chicago's schools, teachers, and students.

We strive for all of our programs to strengthen each student's power to express ideas effectively, creatively, confidently, and in their individual voice by providing them a safe space to be their most creative selves.

Learn more at: www.826chi.org.

ABOUT THE WICKER PARK SECRET AGENT SUPPLY CO.

826CHI shares its space with the Wicker Park Secret Agent Supply Co., a store with a not-so-secret mission. Our unique products encourage creative writing and imaginative play, and trigger new adventures for agents of all ages. Every purchase supports 826CHI's free programming, so visit us at 1276 N Milwaukee Ave in Wicker Park to pick up writing tools, fancy notebooks, assorted fake moustaches and other stellar disguises, books from local publishers, our latest student publications, and much more!

Or, visit us online at www.secretagentsupply.com.

OUR PROGRAMS

826CHI's free programs reach students at every opportunity—in school, after school, in the evenings, and on the weekends.

AFTER-SCHOOL TUTORING AND WRITING

826CHI is packed four afternoons a week with students in first through eighth grade working on their homework and sharpening their creative writing skills. Volunteer tutors help students with any and all homework assignments and lead students in daily creative and expository writing activities. Student writing created during tutoring is published in chapbooks throughout the year, and we frequently host student readings for parents, tutors, families, and the greater 826CHI community.

FIELD TRIPS

On weekday mornings throughout the school year, we host classes from Chicago schools for lively, writing-based Field Trips at our writing center. Teachers may choose from a wide range of programs, such as our Storytelling & Bookmaking Field Trip, which focuses on plot and character development, or "I Remember . . ." Memoir Writing, in which teenage students transform powerful memories into reflective prose.

WORKSHOPS

Designed to foster creativity, strengthen writing skills, and provide students with a forum to execute projects they otherwise might not have the support to undertake, 826CHI Workshops are led by talented volunteers—including published authors, educators, playwrights, chefs, and other artists—on Saturdays and throughout the summer.

TEEN WRITERS STUDIO

826CHI's Teen Writers Studio (or "TWS") is a year-long creative writing workshop that connects high school students to fellow writers, including peers and older professionals in the field. It's open to anyone in 9th-12th grade and welcomes youth from all over the city. TWS members meet twice each month to write together, talk about writing, and produce a literary chapbook each June. If you're into any of the above, this space is for you.

PUBLISHING

At 826CHI, each student is challenged to produce their finest writing, knowing that their words will have the opportunity to be read, laughed at, wept over, or deeply pondered by their family, friends, and folks they may not even know. By the power of a very heavy binding machine, we are able to assemble many of the students' pieces into handsome books in-house. When not laying out, cutting up, and binding at 826CHI, we send special collections of writing (like this one!) to a professional printer with gigantic machines in order to put together a well-bound publication.

OUR STAFF

Kendra Curry-Khanna
Executive Director

Julia Clausen
Data and Impact Associate, Americorps VISTA

Ola Faleti
Development Coordinator

Molly Fannin
Director of Development

Gaby FeBland
Communications Coordinator

Gerardo Galán
Program Coordinator

Waringa Hunja
Publications Coordinator

Mackenzie Lynch
Communications Associate, Americorps VISTA

Natasha Mijares
Program and Evaluation Manager

David Pintor
Volunteer Manager

Molly Sprayregen
Program Coordinator

Tyler Stoltenberg
Operations Manager

Maria Villarreal
Director of Programs

www.ingramcontent.com/pod-product-compliance
Lightning Source LLC
Chambersburg PA
CBHW072120150726
47999CB00005B/2048